For Rafe
MB

For John (aka Jack, aka Dad) and Kathy Berube
KB

The illustrator would like to thank
Javan Mngrezzo for the technical guidance on
the ballet drawings. Any errors are her own.

Text copyright © 2022 by Mac Barnett
Illustrations copyright © 2022 by Kate Berube

First edition 2022

Library of Congress Catalog Card Number pending
ISBN 978-1-5362-0395-0

21 22 23 24 25 26 LGO 10 9 8 7 6 5 4 3 2 1

Printed in Vicenza, Italy

This book was typeset in Cambria.
The illustrations were done in ink and paint
on cold-pressed watercolor paper.

Candlewick Press
99 Dover Street
Somerville, Massachusetts 02144

www.candlewick.com

JOHN'S TURN

Mac Barnett

illustrated by Kate Berube

CANDLEWICK PRESS

ON FRIDAYS there's Assembly.
It's in the morning, before class.
We sit in the cafeteria, so it still smells like breakfast.

Mr. Ross does announcements.
Sometimes there's a guest.
And then, if we're good, at the end,
one of us gets to do something for the whole school.

A performance.
It's called "Sharing Gifts."
A lot of us think that's a kind of dumb name,
but we also think Sharing Gifts is the best.

Last week Tina played tuba.

Once Jesse did magic tricks.
That was cool, but it was hard to see his cards from the back.

Carla told us some jokes.

Today was John's turn.

John brought two bags to school,
his backpack and one with his Sharing Gifts stuff.
He was quiet at breakfast. We knew why.
He was nervous.

During announcements, John prepared.
He was hidden behind a big blue curtain.
He unzipped his bag and changed into
his clothes.
He put on a white leotard.
He put on black pants.
He put on black slippers.

Then he was ready.

Behind the blue curtain,
John sat down and waited till it was his turn.
Mr. Ross reminded us permission slips were due Monday.
We all sang a song.

Then he introduced John.

"What's John gonna do?"
Andre asked without raising his hand.
Mr. Ross looked at his paper.
"He's doing a dance."
"Cool," Andre said.
He never raises his hand.

The blue curtain moved,
then John came onto the stage.
We could tell that his heart was beating real fast.

Mr. Ross pressed play.
The music was strings,
violins and things,
and then maybe flutes.

Someone said, "How the heck do you dance to that?"
(It was probably Tiffany.)

A bunch of kids laughed.
Mrs. K. shushed the crowd.

Then it was John's turn.

He danced.

Then John stood still.

He took a bow, breathing hard,

and he looked out at us.

Then it was our turn.

We clapped.